MARCUS PFISTER is the author of the phenomenally successful Rainbow Fish series, as well as many other books for children. He has worked as a graphic artist, a sculptor, a painter, and a photographer as well as a children's book creator.

North
South

MARCUS PFISTER was born in Bern, Switzerland. After studying at the Art School of Bern, he apprenticed as a graphic designer and worked in an advertising agency before becoming self-employed in 1984. His debut picture book, *The Sleepy Owl*, was published by NorthSouth in 1986, but his big breakthrough came six years later with *The Rainbow Fish*. Today, Marcus has illustrated over 65 books, which have been translated into more than 60 languages and received countless international awards. He lives with his wife, Debora, and his children in Bern.

First published in the United States, Great Britain, Canada, Australia, and New Zealand in 2012 by NorthSouth Books Inc., an imprint of NordSüd Verlag AG, CH-8050 Zürich, Switzerland.
Distributed in the United States by NorthSouth Books Inc., New York 10016.
First paperback edition published in Great Britain, Australia and New Zealand in 2012.
Library of Congress Cataloging-in-Publication Data is available.
Printed in China 2021

ISBN: 978-0-7358-4082-9 (trade edition)
3 5 7 9 11 · 12 10 8 6 4
ISBN: 978-0-7358-4085-0 (paperback edition)
5 7 9 11 13 15 · 14 12 10 8 6

www.northsouth.com
Meet Marcus Pfister at www.marcuspfister.ch.

FSC
www.fsc.org
MIX
Paper from
responsible sources
FSC® C007972

Marcus Pfister

Good Night, Little
RAINBOW FISH

North
South

The Little Rainbow Fish couldn't sleep.
His eyes simply wouldn't close. He tossed and
turned in his watery bed of plants.

"I can't get to sleep," moaned Little Rainbow Fish.

"What's the trouble, darling?" asked Mommy.

"It's so dark."

"Don't be afraid!" said Mommy. "I'll send for the lantern fish. He'll shine his light for you until you fall asleep. Good night, Little Rainbow Fish."

"Could you stay with me for a while, Mommy?"
"I'll never leave your side, darling."
"Promise?"
"Cross my rainbow heart!"

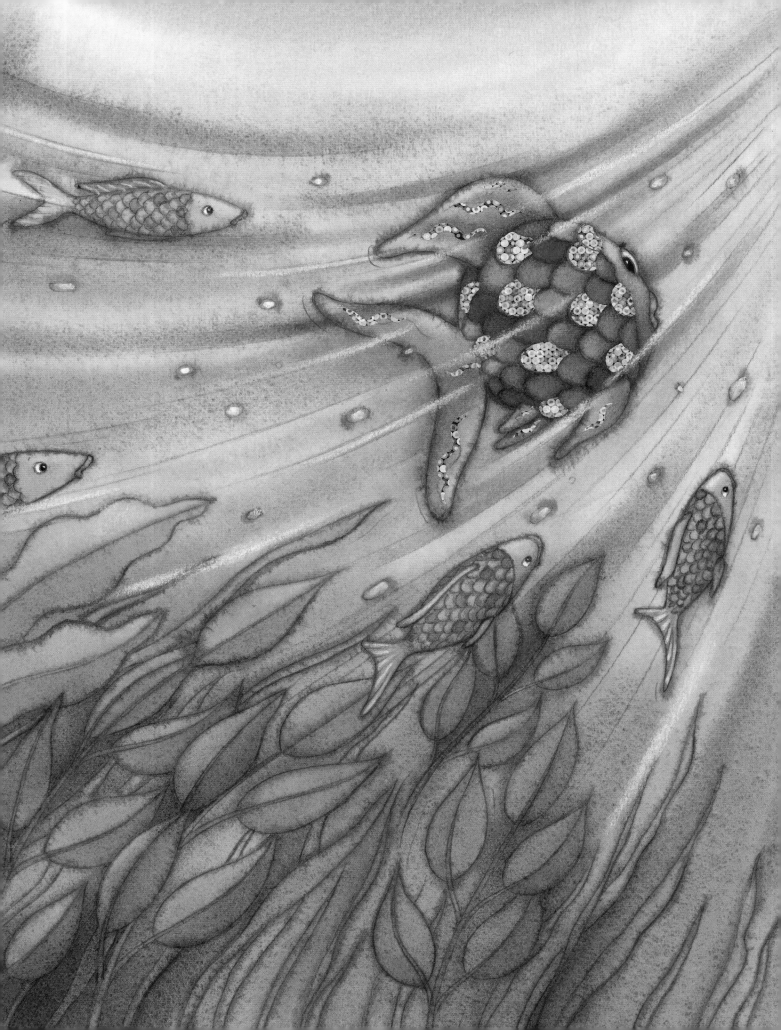

"But suppose the tide comes and takes me away?"

"Then I'll follow you faster than a swordfish can swim and bring you safely home again."

"And suppose I lose my way in
an octopus's cloud of ink?"

"Then I'll search for you, blow away
the black cloud, and take you home."

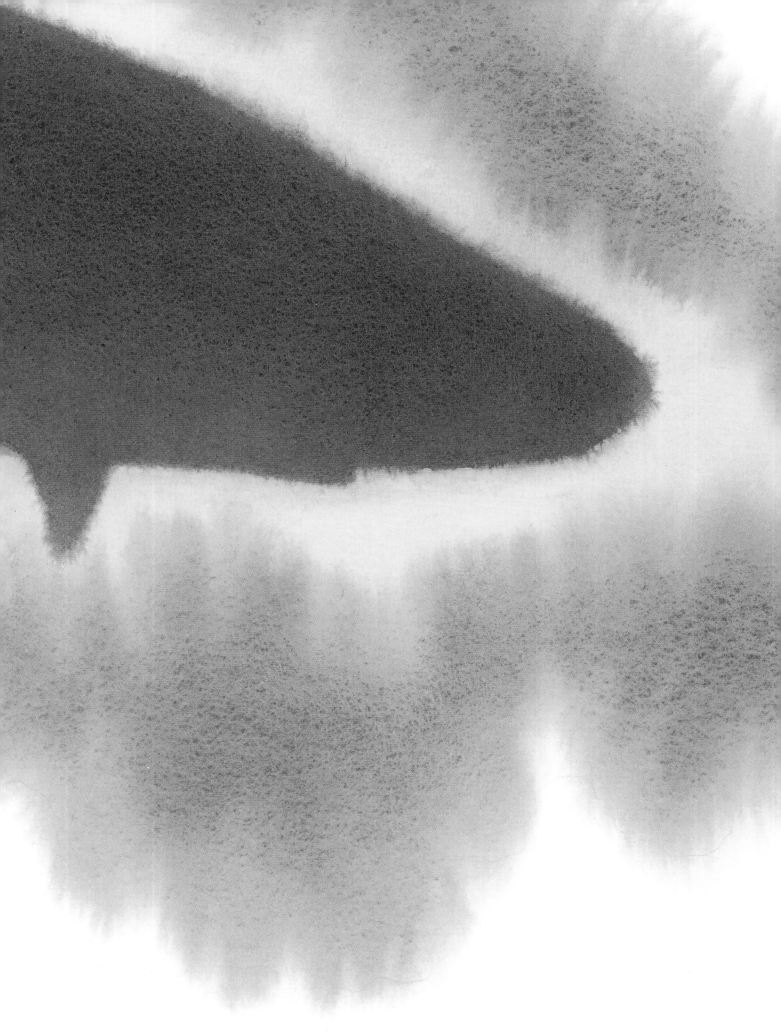

"And suppose a monster fish
comes to gobble me up?"

"Then the monster fish will have to face me first! And I'll give him such a fright that he'll swim away and never come back."

"And suppose I get caught in the arms of a poisonous jellyfish?"

"Then I'll nurse you until you're well
again, and the jellyfish will
get a nasty surprise."

"And suppose I have a bad dream tonight?"

"Then I'll take you in my fins and hold you very, very tight. Good night, darling."

"Good night, Mommy," murmured Little Rainbow Fish, and then he happily fell asleep.

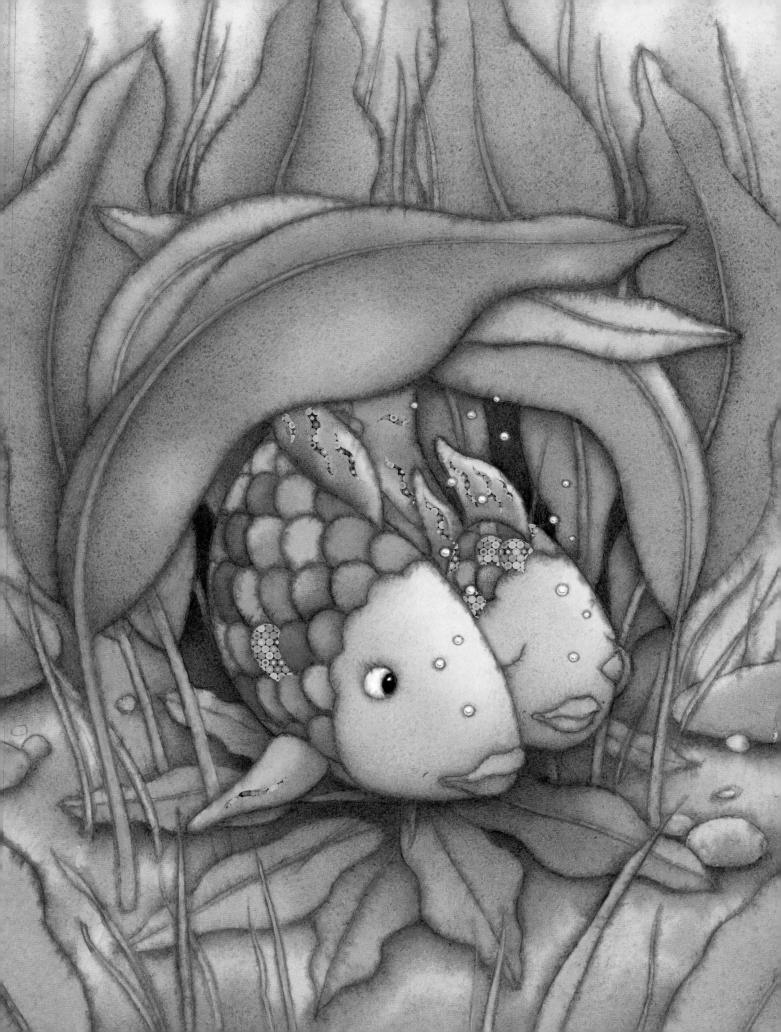

Read all the Rainbow Fish Adventures: